Christopher Changes His Name

ITAH SADU   ROY CONDY

FIREFLY BOOKS

For my daughter Sojourner Monifa
and my niece Adeyianka.
Beautiful with life, and light, and love.
To Harold Hoyte — The Nation —
and to Marie Mumford, thanks for the inspiration.
—Itah

A FIREFLY BOOK

Published in the U.S. in 1998 by:
Firefly Books (U.S.) Inc.
P.O. Box 1338
Ellicott Station
Buffalo, New York 14207

Cataloguing in Publication Data

Sadu, Itah, 1961-
    Christopher changes his name

ISBN 1-55209-216-X (bound) ISBN 1-55209-214-3 (pbk.)

I. Condy, Roy. II. Title.

PS8587.A242C47 1998   jC813'.54   C97-932070-4
PZ7.S22Ch 1998

Original text by Itah Sadu copyright © 1996.
Original illustrations by Roy Condy copyright © 1996.
Published by arrangement with North Winds Press.

6 5 4 3 2 1   Printed and bound in Canada   8 9 / 9

Christopher was on his way home from school. He was
having a bad day. The sky was a dark, angry grey-blue and it
was raining all over everyone. Christopher splashed through
the puddles feeling just as miserable as the day.

He was in a bad mood because he hated his name. It wasn't a special name. Millions of people all over the world had that name. There were eleven Christophers in his school and three in his class! Every time the teacher said "Christopher," they would all answer. It had happened at least four times that day. It drove him crazy!

3

Now it so happened that Christopher's aunt — Aunt Gail — she was visiting from Trinidad and Tobago. Aunt Gail was a fabulous storyteller. She told stories about a man called Tiger. Now Tiger, he could eat five hot red peppers and ask for ten more! He was so strong he could carry his cows on his shoulders to market. In the night, he walked so softly and silently that the people in the village, they called him Tiger.

Christopher, he was fascinated! He wanted to be strong and silent like Tiger.

And right then and there, Christopher changed his name to Tiger.

He rushed here and he rushed there and he told everyone, "My new name is Tiger." He began to walk softly and quietly like a tiger. He even carried the books for all the people in his class, because he was so strong. And everyone here and there, they all started calling him Tiger.

All except his teacher, Ms Mumford. She called him Christopher Mulamba.

A few weeks later Tiger went to the Science Fair with his mother. It was happening — there were windmills and engines and all kinds of experiments all over the place. And on one table was a picture labeled The Real McCoy.

"Mom," Tiger asked, "who is The Real McCoy?"

"Why, that's Elijah McCoy. He was an important African-American scientist."

"He was so smart, he invented a way to make machines oil themselves."

Well! Tiger, he wanted to be a scientist! He wanted to be important like The Real McCoy. It was far more important to be important. Right then and there, Tiger changed his name to The Real McCoy.

And he rushed here and he rushed there, and he told everyone, "My name is The Real McCoy." Back at school, all through lunch, all through recess, he experimented with cups and paperclips and pencils, and who knows what! It was so cool, the whole class joined in. One boy, he called

himself Charles Darwin. A girl called herself Sally Ride.
And everyone here and there, they all started calling Tiger
The Real McCoy.

All except his teacher, Ms Mumford. She called him
Christopher Mulamba.

Late one evening, The Real McCoy was watching television with his family. There was excitement in the house. The Chicago Bulls were playing. The Real McCoy's heart was beating fast as he watched Michael Jordan swoop and soar. He was moving so fast, sometimes all you could see was his number, 23, flying all around.

The Real McCoy
wanted to fly too! He
wanted the crowds to cheer
for him. Being important didn't
seem so important anymore. But
being famous did! He wanted to be 23. He wanted it
bad. Right then and there, The Real McCoy changed his
name. He dribbled and dunked all over the place, driving
everyone crazy. And everyone here and there, they
all started calling him 23.

All except his teacher,
Ms Mumford. She called him
Christopher Mulamba.

July 24 came, and it was 23's birthday. He woke up and
there was a big card next to his bed. It was from his
grandmother. It said "To Christopher, a very special child.
May you soar and touch the sky."

23, he felt good. Because in the card was a check for a
hundred and fifty dollars. Yes! He would open his own
new bank account — yes! He would even buy a number
23 jacket. Yes!

That very same day, 23 and his mother went to the bank. 23 rushed up to the bank manager.

"Hi!" he said. "I'm 23 and I'm here to open an account! And this is my mother."

The bank manager looked at him and said, "How do you do, 23? Very glad to meet you." He showed them into his office and he gave them some forms to fill out.

Suddenly, the bank manager frowned. He looked at the check and he looked at 23, and he looked at the check and he looked at 23. Then he said, "We've got a problem here. This check is made out to Christopher Mulamba, but your name is 23."

23 looked at the bank manager and he looked at his mother. "Yeah — I — I'm 23, but I'm really — I really am Christopher. *Mom!*"

19

And his mother said, "I think you'd better handle this yourself, 23."

What was he going to do? He looked inside his backpack, but his notebooks, his school books, everything now said 23. He was in a real mess. He needed some identification. Fast.

Just then, who should come through the bank door but his best friends, Jason and Shea. He rushed up to them and said, "Hi, guys. What's my name?"

And they said, "23, of course!"

The whole world was against him! He *was* Christopher Mulamba. It was a special name, after all — it was the only name that could cash that check! What was he going to do? Then he looked up and saw someone else entering the bank. Ms Mumford. Yes!

"Hi, Ms Mumford!" Christopher said.

Ms Mumford, she looked over at him and she thought

to herself, *Hmm. There's that child with all the names. I think I'll humor him today.*

"How are you doing, 23?"

BANG! BANG!

Christopher went flying back to his chair, sat down hard, and banged his foot against the bank manager's desk. His mother looked over at him and she said, "Stop banging your foot, 23."

BANG! BANG!

But he banged and he banged and he banged. He was Christopher! Why didn't the bank manager believe him? How could he get himself out of this?

"Stop banging your foot," his mother said. But he didn't stop.

He had to get that money. He was Christopher!
He banged louder and he banged louder, until his
mother said, "*Christopher Kwame Mulamba*, I said
stop banging that foot!"

Christopher Kwame Mulamba, he looked at the bank
manager and smiled. *Gotcha!* Then he carefully signed
the check.

And do you know what? From that day on, Christopher
never, ever, ever once changed his name.

Because it was just so special!